RUMPOLE AND THE
YOUNGER GENERATION

JOHN
MORTIMER

RUMPOLE AND THE
YOUNGER GENERATION

penguin books

PENGUIN BOOKS
Published by the Penguin Group
Penguin Books USA Inc., 375 Hudson Street,
New York, New York 10014, U.S.A.
Penguin Books Ltd, 27 Wrights Lane,
London W8 5TZ, England
Penguin Books Australia Ltd, Ringwood,
Victoria, Australia
Penguin Books Canada Ltd, 10 Alcorn Avenue,
Toronto, Ontario, Canada M4V 3B2
Penguin Books (N.Z.) Ltd, 182–190 Wairau Road,
Auckland 10, New Zealand

Penguin Books Ltd, Registered Offices:
Harmondsworth, Middlesex, England

Published in Penguin Books 1995

"Rumpole and the Younger Generation" appears in *Rumpole of the
Bailey* by John Mortimer, Penguin Books, 1978

ISBN 0 14 60.0006 4

Printed in the United States of America

RUMPOLE AND THE
YOUNGER GENERATION

I, Horace Rumpole, barrister at law, sixty-eight next birthday, Old Bailey hack, husband to Mrs Hilda Rumpole (known to me only as She Who Must Be Obeyed) and father to Nicholas Rumpole (lecturer in social studies at the University of Baltimore, I have always been extremely proud of Nick); I, who have a mind full of old murders, legal anecdotes and memorable fragments of the *Oxford Book of English Verse* (Sir Arthur Quiller-Couch's edition) together with a dependable knowledge of bloodstains, blood groups, fingerprints, and forgery by typewriter; I, who am now the oldest member of my chambers, take up my pen at this advanced age during a lull in business (there's not much crime about, all the best villains seem to be off on holiday in the Costa Brava), in order to write my reconstructions of some of my recent triumphs (including a number of recent disasters) in the courts of law, hoping thereby to turn a bob or two which won't be immediately grabbed by the taxman, or my clerk Henry, or by She Who Must Be Obeyed, and perhaps give some sort of entertainment to those who, like myself, have found in British justice a lifelong subject of harmless fun.

When I first considered putting pen to paper in this matter of my life, I thought I must begin with the great cases of my comparative youth, the Penge Bungalow Murders, where I gained an acquittal alone and without a leader, or the

Great Brighton Benefit Club Forgery, which I contrived to win by reason of my exhaustive study of typewriters. In these cases I was, for a brief moment, in the Public Eye, or at least my name seemed almost a permanent feature of the *News of the World*, but when I come to look back on that period of my life at the Bar it all seems to have happened to another Rumpole, an eager young barrister whom I can scarcely recognize and whom I am not at all sure I would like, at least not enough to spend a whole book with him.

I am not a public figure now, so much has to be admitted; but some of the cases I shall describe, the wretched business of the Honourable Member, for instance, or the charge of murder brought against the youngest, and barmiest, of the appalling Delgardo brothers, did put me back on the front page of the *News of the World* (and even got me a few inches in *The Times*). But I suppose I have become pretty well known, if not something of a legend, round the Old Bailey, in Pommeroy's Wine Bar in Fleet Street, in the robing-room at London Sessions and in the cells at Brixton Prison. They know me there for never pleading guilty, for chain-smoking small cigars, and for quoting Wordsworth when they least expect it. Such notoriety will not long survive my not-to-be-delayed trip to Golders Green Crematorium. Barristers' speeches vanish quicker than Chinese dinners, and even the greatest victory in court rarely survives longer than the next Sunday's papers.

To understand the full effect on my family life, however, of
that case which I have called 'Rumpole and the Younger

Generation', it is necessary to know a little of my past and the long years that led up to my successful defence of Jim Timson, the sixteen-year-old sprig, the young hopeful, and apple of the eye of the Timsons, a huge and industrious family of South London villains. As this case was, by and large, a family matter, it is important that you should understand my family.

My father, the Reverend Wilfred Rumpole, was a Church of England clergyman who, in early middle age, came reluctantly to the conclusion that he no longer believed any one of the Thirty-nine Articles. As he was not fitted by character or training for any other profession, however, he had to soldier on in his living in Croydon and by a good deal of scraping and saving he was able to send me as a boarder to a minor public school on the Norfolk coast. I later went to Keble College, Oxford, where I achieved a dubious third in law – you will discover during the course of these memoirs that, although I only feel truly alive and happy in law courts, I have a singular distaste for the law. My father's example, and the number of theological students I met at Keble, gave me an early mistrust of clergymen whom I have always found to be most unsatisfactory witnesses. If you call a clergyman in mitigation, the old darling can be guaranteed to add at least a year to the sentence.

When I first went to the Bar, I entered the chambers of C. H. Wystan. Wystan had a moderate practice, acquired rather by industry than talent, and a strong disinclination to look at the photographs in murder cases, being particularly squeamish on the fascinating subject of blood. He also had a daughter, Hilda Wystan as was, now Mrs Hilda Rumpole and She Who Must Be Obeyed. I was ambitious in those days. I did my best to cultivate Wystan's clerk Albert, and I started to get a good deal of criminal work. I did what was expected of me and spent happy hours round the Bailey and Sessions and my fame grew in criminal circles; at the end of the day I would take Albert for a drink in Pommeroy's Wine Bar. We got on extremely well and he would always recommend 'his Mr Rumpole' if a solicitor rang up with a particularly tricky indecent assault or a nasty case of receiving stolen property.

There is no point in writing your memoirs unless you are prepared to be completely candid, and I must confess that, in the course of a long life, I have been in love on several occasions. I am sure that I loved Miss Porter, the shy and nervous, but at times liberated daughter of Septimus Porter, my Oxford tutor in Roman Law. In fact we were engaged to be married, but the engagement had to be broken off because of Miss Porter's early death. I often think about her, and of the different course my home life might have taken, for Miss Porter was in no way a girl born to command, or expect, implicit obedience. During my service with the ground staff of the RAF I undoubtedly became helplessly smitten with the charms of an extremely warm-hearted and gallant officer in the WAFFs by the name of Miss Bobby O'Keefe, but I was no match for the wings of a Pilot Officer, as appeared on the chest of a certain Sam 'Three Fingers' Dogherty. During my conduct of a case, which I shall describe in a later story which I have called 'Rumpole and the Alternative Society', I once again felt a hopeless and almost feverish stirring of passion for a young woman who was determined to talk her way into Holloway Prison. My relationship with Hilda Wystan was rather different.

To begin with, she seemed part of life in chambers. She was always interested in the law and ambitious, first for her widowed father, and then, when he proved himself unlikely Lord Chancellor material, for me. She often dropped in for tea on her way home from shopping, and Wystan used to invite me in for a cup. One year I was detailed off to be her partner at an Inns of Court ball. There it became clear to me that I was expected to marry Hilda; it seemed a step in my career like getting a brief in the Court of Appeal, or doing a murder. When she proposed to me, as she did over a glass of claret cup after an energetic waltz, Hilda made it clear that, when old Wystan finally retired, she expected to see me Head of Chambers. I, who have never felt at a loss for a word in court, found absolutely nothing to say. In that silence the matter was concluded.

So now you must picture Hilda and me twenty-five years later, with a son at that same east-coast public school which I just managed to afford from the fruits of crime, in our matrimonial home at 25B Froxbury Mansions, Gloucester Road. (A mansion flat is a misleading description of that cavernous and underheated area which Hilda devotes so much of her energy to keeping shipshape, not to say Bristol fashion.) We were having breakfast, and, between bites of toast, I was reading my brief for that day, an Old Bailey trial of the sixteen-year-old Jim Timson charged with robbery with violence, he having allegedly taken part in a wage snatch on a couple of elderly butchers: an escapade planned in the playground of the local comprehensive. As so often happens, the poet Wordsworth, that old sheep of the Lake District, sprang immediately to mind, and I gave tongue to his lines, well knowing that they must only serve to irritate She Who Must Be Obeyed: '"Trailing clouds of glory do we come/ From God, who is our home;/Heaven lies about us in our infancy!"'

I looked at Hilda. She was impassively demolishing a boiled egg. I also noticed that she was wearing a hat, as if prepared to set out upon some expedition. I decided to give her a little more Wordsworth, prompted by my reading the story of the boy Timson: '"Shades of the prison-house begin to close/Upon the growing boy."'

Hilda spoke at last.

'Rumpole, you're not talking about your son, I hope. You're never referring to Nick . . .'

'"Shades of the prison-house begin to close"? Not round our son, of course. Not round Nick. Shades of the public school have grown round him, the thousand-quid-a-year remand home.'

Hilda always thought it indelicate to refer to the subject of school fees, as if being at Mulstead were a kind of unsolicited honour for Nick. She became increasingly business-like.

'He's breaking up this morning.'

'Shades of the prison-house begin to open up for the holidays.'

6   'Nick has to be met at 11.15 at Liverpool Street and given

lunch. When he went back to school you promised him a show. You haven't forgotten?'

Hilda was clearing away the plates rapidly. To tell the truth I had forgotten the date of Nick's holidays; but I let her assume I had a long-planned treat laid on for him.

'Of course I haven't forgotten. The only show I can offer him is a Robbery with Violence at the Old Bailey. I wish I could lay on a murder. Nick's always so enjoyed my murders.'

It was true. On one distant half-term Nick had sat in on the Peckham Billiard Hall Stabbing, and enjoyed it a great deal more than *Treasure Island*.

'I must fly! Daddy gets so crotchety if anyone's late. And he does love his visits.'

Hilda removed my half-empty coffee cup.

'Our father which art in Horsham. Give my respects to the old sweetheart.'

It had also slipped my mind that old C. H. Wystan was laid up with a dicky ticker in Horsham General Hospital. The hat was, no doubt, a clue I should have followed. Hilda usually goes shopping in a headscarf. By now she was at the door, and looking disapproving.

'"Old sweetheart" is hardly how you used to talk of the Head of your chambers.'

'Somehow I can never remember to call the Head of my chambers "Daddy".'

The door was open. Hilda was making a slow and effective exit.

'Tell Nick I'll be back in good time to get his supper.'

'Your wish is my command!' I muttered in my best imitation of a slave out of *Chu Chin Chow*. She chose to ignore it.

'And try not to leave the kitchen looking as though it's been hit by a bomb.'

'I hear, oh Master of the Blue Horizons.' I said this with a little more confidence, as she had by now started off on her errand of mercy, and I added, for good measure, 'She Who Must Be Obeyed'.

I had finished my breakfast, and was already thinking how much easier life with the Old Bailey judge was than marriage.

Soon after I finished my breakfast with Hilda, and made plans to meet my son at the start of his holidays from school, Fred Timson, star of a dozen court appearances, was seeing *his* son in the cells under the Old Bailey as the result of a specially arranged visit. I know he brought the boy his best jacket, which his mother had taken specially to the cleaners, and insisted on his putting on a tie. I imagine he told him that they had the best 'brief' in the business to defend him, Mr Rumpole having always done wonders for the Timson family. I know that Fred told young Jim to stand up straight in the witness-box and remember to call the judge 'my Lord' and not show his ignorance by coming out with any gaffe such as 'your Honour', or 'Sir'. The world, that day, was full of fathers showing appropriate and paternal concern.

The robbery with which Jim Timson was charged was an
exceedingly simple one. At about 7 p.m. one Friday evening,

the date being 16 September, the two elderly Brixton butchers, Mr Cadwallader and Mr Lewis Stein, closed their shop in Bombay Road and walked with their week's takings round the corner to a narrow alley-way known as Green's Passage, where their grey Austin van was parked. When they got to the van they found that the front tyres had been deflated. They stooped to inspect the wheels and, as they did so they were attacked by a number of boys, some armed with knives and one flourishing a cricket stump. Luckily, neither of the butchers was hurt, but the attaché case containing their money was snatched.

Chief Inspector 'Persil' White, the old darling in whose territory this outrage had been committed, arrested Jim Timson. All the other boys got clean away, but no doubt because he came from a family well known, indeed almost embarrassingly familiar, to the Chief Inspector, and because of certain rumours in the school playground, he was charged and put on an identity parade. The butchers totally failed to identify him; but, when he was in the remand centre, young Jim, according to the evidence, had boasted to another boy of having 'done the butchers'.

As I thought about this case on my way to the Temple that morning, it occurred to me that Jim Timson was a year younger than my son, but that he had got a step further than Nick in following his father's profession. I had always hoped Nick would go into the law, and, as I say, he seemed to thoroughly enjoy my murders.

In the clerk's room in chambers Albert was handing out the 9 work for the day: rather as a trainer sends his string of horses out on the gallops. I looked round the familiar faces, my friend George Frobisher, who is an old sweetheart but an absolutely hopeless advocate (he can't ask for costs without writing down what he's going to say), was being fobbed off with a Nuisance at Kingston County Court. Young Erskine-Brown, who wears striped shirts and what I believe are known as 'Chelsea boots', was turning up his well-bred nose at an Indecent Assault at Lambeth (a job I'd have bought Albert a double claret in Pommeroy's for at his age) and saying he would prefer a little civil work, adding that he was sick to death of crime.

I have very little patience with Erskine-Brown.

'A person who is tired of crime,' I told him quite candidly, 'is tired of life.'

'Your Dangerous and Careless at Clerkenwell is on the mantelpiece, Mr Hoskins,' Albert said.

Hoskins is a gloomy fellow with four daughters; he's always lurking about our clerk's room looking for cheques. As I've told him often enough crime doesn't pay, or at any rate not for a very long time.

When a young man called MacLay had asked in vain for a brief I invited him to take a note for me down at the Old Bailey. At least he'd get a wig on and not spend a miserable day unemployed in chambers. Our oldest member, Uncle Tom (very few of us remember that his name is T. C. Rowley) also asked Albert if there were any briefs for him, not in the least expecting to find one. To my certain knowl-edge, Uncle Tom hasn't appeared in court for fifteen years, when he managed to lose an undefended divorce case, but, as he lives with a widowed sister, a lady of such reputed ferocity that she makes She Who Must Be Obeyed sound like Mrs Tiggywinkle, he spends most of his time in chambers. He looks remarkably well for seventy-eight.

'You aren't actually *expecting* a brief, Uncle Tom, are you?' Erskine-Brown asked. I can't like Erskine-Brown.

'Time was,' Uncle Tom started one of his reminiscences of life in our chambers. 'Time was when I had more briefs in my corner of the mantelpiece, Erskine-Brown, than you've seen in the whole of your short career at the Bar. Now,' he was opening a brown envelope, 'I only get invitations to insure my life. It's a little late for that.'

Albert told me that the Robbery was not before 11.30 before Mr Justice Everglade in Number One Court. He also told me who was prosecuting, none other than the tall, elegant figure with the silk handkerchief and gold wristwatch, leaning against the mantelpiece and negligently reading a large cheque from the Director of Public Prosecutions, Guthrie Featherstone, MP. He removed the silk handkerchief, dabbed the end of his nose and his small moustache and asked in that voice which comes over so charmingly, saying nothing much about any important topic of the day in *World at One*, 'Agin me, Rumpole? Are you agin me?' He covered a slight yawn with the handkerchief before returning it to his breast pocket. 'Just come from an all-night sitting down at the House. I don't suppose your robbery'll be much of a worry.'

'Only, possibly, to young Jim Timson,' I told him, and

then gave Albert his orders for the day. 'Mrs Rumpole's gone down to see her father in Horsham.'

'How is Wystan? No better, is he?' Uncle Tom sounded as gently pleased as all old men do when they hear news of illness in others.

'Much the same, Uncle Tom, thank you. And young Nick, my son . . .'

'Master Nick?' Albert had always been fond of Nick, and looked forward to putting him through his paces when the time came for him to join our stable in chambers.

'He's breaking up today. So he'll need meeting at Liverpool Street. Then he can watch a bit of the robbery.'

'We're going to have your son in the audience? I'd better be brilliant.' Guthrie Featherstone now moved from the fireplace.

'You needn't bother, old darling. It's his Dad he comes to see.'

'Oh, *touché*, Rumpole! *Distinctement touché!*'

Featherstone talks like that. Then he invited me to walk down to the Bailey with him. Apparently he was still capable of movement and didn't need a stretcher, even after a sleepless night with the Gas Mains Enabling Bill, or whatever it was.

We walked together down Fleet Street and into Ludgate Circus, Featherstone wearing his overcoat with the velvet collar and little round bowler hat, I puffing a small cigar and with my old mac flapping in the wind; I discovered that the gentleman beside me was quietly quizzing me about my career at the Bar.

'You've been at this game a long while, Rumpole,' Featherstone announced. I didn't disagree with him, and then he went on.

'You never thought of taking silk?'

'Rumpole, QC?' I almost burst out laughing. 'Not on your Nelly. Rumpole "Queer Customer". That's what they'd be bound to call me.'

'I'm sure you could, with your seniority.' I had no idea then, of exactly what this Featherstone was after. I gave him my view of QCs in general.

'Perhaps, if I played golf with the right judges, or put up for Parliament, they might make me an artificial silk, or, at any rate, a nylon.' It was at that point I realized I had put up a bit of a black. 'Sorry. I forgot. You *did* put up for Parliament.'

'Yes. You never thought of Rumpole, QC?' Featherstone had apparently taken no offence.

'Never,' I told him. 'I have the honour to be an Old Bailey hack! That's quite enough for me.'

At which point we turned up into Newgate Street and there it was in all its glory, touched by a hint of early spring sunshine, the Old Bailey, a stately law court, decreed by the City Fathers, an Edwardian palace, with an extensive modern extension to deal with the increase in human fallibility. There was the dome and the Blindfold Lady. Well, it's much better she doesn't see *all* that's going on. That, in fact, was our English version of the *palais de justice*, complete with murals, marble statues and underground accommodation for some of the choicest villains in London.

Terrible things go on down the Bailey – horrifying things. 13

Why is it I never go in the revolving door without a thrill of pleasure, a slight tremble of excitement? Why does it seem a much *jollier* place than my flat in Gloucester Road under the strict rule of She Who Must Be Obeyed? These are questions which may only be partly answered in the course of these memoirs.

At the time when I was waving a cheerful umbrella at Harry, the policeman in the revolving door of the Old Bailey extension, my wife Hilda was at her Daddy's bedside at the Horsham General arranging her dozen early daffs and gently probing, so she told me that evening, on the subject of his future, and mine.

'I'll have to give up, you know. I can't go on forever. Crocked up, I'm afraid,' said Wystan.

'Nonsense, Daddy. You'll go on for years.'

I imagine Hilda did her best to sound bracing, whilst putting the daffs firmly in their place.

'No, Hilda. No. They'll have to start looking for another Head of Chambers.'

This gave Hilda her opportunity. 'Rumpole's the senior man. Apart from Uncle Tom and he doesn't really practise nowadays.'

'Your husband the senior man.' Wystan looked back on a singularly uneventful life. 'How time flies! I recall when he was the junior man. My pupil.'

'You said he was the best youngster on bloodstains you'd ever known.' Hilda was doing her best for me.

'Rumpole! Yes, your husband was pretty good on bloodstains. Shaky, though, on the law of landlord and tenant. What sort of practice has Rumpole now?'

'I believe . . . Today it's the Old Bailey.' Hilda was plumping pillows, doing her best to sound casual. And her father showed no particular enthusiasm for my place of work.

'It's always the Old Bailey, isn't it?'

'Most of the time. Yes. I suppose so.'

'Not a frightfully good *address*, the Old Bailey. Not exactly the SW 1 of the legal profession.'

Sensing that Daddy would have thought better of me if I'd been in the Court of Appeal or the Chancery Division, Hilda told me she thought of a master stroke.

'Oh, Rumpole only went down to the Bailey because it's a family he knows. It seems they've got a young boy in trouble.'

This appealed to Daddy, he gave one of his bleak smiles which amount to no more than a brief withdrawal of lips from the dentures.

'Son gone wrong?' he said. 'Very sad that. Especially if he comes of a really good family.'

That really good family, the Timsons, was out in force and waiting outside Number One Court by the time I had got on the fancy dress, yellowing horse-hair wig, gown become more than a trifle tattered over the years, and bands round the neck that Albert ought to have sent to the laundry after last week's Death by Dangerous Driving. As I looked at the Timson clan assembled, I thought the best thing about them was the amount of work of a criminal nature they had brought into chambers. They were all dressed for the occasion, the men in dark blazers, suede shoes and grey flannels; the ladies in tight-fitting suits, high heels and elaborately piled hairdos. I had never seen so many ex-clients together at one time.

'Mr Rumpole.'

'Ah, Bernard! You're instructing me.'

Mr Bernard, the solicitor, was a thirtyish, perpetually smiling man in a pinstriped suit. He regarded criminals with something of the naïve fervour with which young girls think of popular entertainers. Had I known the expression at the time I would have called him a grafters' 'groupie'.

'I'm always your instructing solicitor in a Timson case, Mr Rumpole.' Mr Bernard beamed and Fred Timson, a kindly man and most innocent robber, stepped out of the ranks to do the honours.

'Nothing but the best for the Timsons, best solicitor and best barrister going. You know my wife Vi?'

Young Jim's mother seemed full of confidence. As I took her hand, I remembered I had got Vi off on a handling charge after the Croydon Bank Raid. Well, there was really no evidence.

'Uncle Cyril.' Fred introduced the plumpish uncle with the small moustache whom I was sure I remembered. What was *his* last outing exactly? Carrying house-breaking instruments by night?

'Uncle Dennis. You remember Den, surely, Mr Rumpole?'

I did. Den's last little matter was an alleged conspiracy to forge log books.

'And Den's Doris.'

Aunty Doris came at me in a blur of henna-ed hair and darkish perfume. What was Doris's last indiscretion? Could it have been receiving a vast quantity of stolen scampi? Acquitted by a majority, at least I was sure of that.

'And yours truly. Frederick Timson. The boy's father.'

Regrettable, but we had a slip-up with Fred's last spot of bother. I was away with flu, George Frobisher took it over and he got three years. He must've only just got out.

'So, Mr Rumpole. You know the whole family.'

A family to breed from, the Timsons. Must almost keep the Old Bailey going single-handed.

'You're going to do your best for our young Jim, I'm sure, Mr Rumpole.'

I didn't find the simple faith of the Timsons that I could secure acquittals in the most unlikely circumstances especially encouraging. But then Jim's mother said something which I was to long remember.

'He's a good boy. He was ever so good to me while Dad was away.'

So that was Jimbo's life. Head of the family at fourteen, when Dad was off on one of his regular visits to Her Majesty.

'It's young Jim's first appearance, like. At the Old Bailey.' Fred couldn't conceal a note of pride. It was Jim boy's Bar Mitzvah, his First Communion.

So we chatted a little about how all the other boys got clean away, which I told them was a bit of luck as none of them would go into the witness-box and implicate Jim, and Bernard pointed out that the identification by the butchers 17 was pretty hopeless. Well, what did he expect? Would you have a photographic impression of the young hopeful who struck you a smart blow on the back of the head with a cricket stump? We talked with that curious suppressed excitement there always is before a trial, however disastrous the outcome may be, and I told them the only thing we had to worry about, as if that were not enough, was Jim's confession to the boy in the remand centre, a youth who rejoiced in the name of Peanuts Molloy.

'Peanuts Molloy! Little grass.' Fred Timson spoke with a deep contempt.

'Old Persil White fitted him up with that one, didn't he?' Uncle Cyril said it as if it were the most natural thing in the world, and only to be expected.

'Chief Detective Inspector White,' Bernard explained.

'Why should the Chief Inspector want to fit up your Jimbo?' It was a question to which I should have known what their answer would be.

'Because he's a Timson, that's why!' said Fred.

'Because he's the apple of our eye, like,' Uncle Den told me, and the boy's mother added:

'Being as he's the baby of the family.'

'Old Persil'd fit up his mother if it'd get him a smile from his Super.' As Fred said this the Chief Inspector himself, grey-haired and avuncular, walked by in plain clothes, with a plain-clothes sergeant.

'Morning, Chief Inspector,' Fred carried on without drawing breath.

'Morning, Fred. Morning, Mrs Timson.' The Chief Inspector greeted the family with casual politeness – after all, they were part of his daily work – and Vi sniffed back a 'Good morning, Chief Inspector.'

'Mr Timson. We'll shift our ground. Remove, good friends.'

Like Hamlet, after seeing the ghost, I thought it was better to continue our conference in private. So we went and sat round a table in the canteen, and, when we had sorted out who took how many lumps, and which of them could do with a choc roll or a cheese sandwich, the family gave me the lowdown on the chief prosecution witness.

'The Chief Inspector put that little grass Peanuts Molloy into Jim's painting class at the remand centre.' Fred had no doubt about it.

'Jim apparently poured out his soul to Peanuts.' The evidence sounded, to my old ears, completely convincing, and Bernard read us a snatch from his file.

'We planned to do the old blokes from the butcher's and grab the wages . . .'

'That,' I reminded the assembled company, 'is what Peanuts will say Jim told him.'

'You think I'd bring Jim up to talk in the Nick like that? The Timsons ain't stupid!' Fred was outraged, and Vi, pursing her lips in a sour gesture of wounded respectability, added, 'His Dad's always told him. Never say a word to anyone you're banged up with – bound to be a grass.'

One by one, Aunty Doris, Uncle Den and Uncle Cyril added their support.

'That's right. Fred's always brought the boy up proper.

Like the way he should be. He'd never speak about the crime, not to anyone he was banged up with.'

'Specially not to one of the Molloys!'

'The Molloys!' Vi spoke for the Timsons, and with deep hatred. 'Noted grasses. That family always has been.'

'The Molloys is beyond the pale. Well known for it.' Aunty Doris nodded her henna-ed topknot wisely.

'Peanuts's Grandad shopped my old father in the Streatham Co-op Robbery. Pre-war, that was.'

I had a vague memory then of what Fred Timson was talking about. The Streatham Co-op case, one of my better briefs – a long case with not much honour shown among thieves, as far as I could remember.

'Then you can understand, Mr Rumpole. No Timson would ever speak to a Molloy.'

'So you're sure Jimbo never said anything to Peanuts?' I was wondering exactly how I could explain the deep, but not particularly creditable, origins of this family hostility to the jury.

'I give you my word, Mr Rumpole. Ain't that enough for you? No Timson would ever speak to a Molloy. Not under any circumstances.'

There were not many matters on which I would take Fred Timson's word, but the history of the Streatham Co-op case came back to me, and this was one of them.

It's part of the life of an Old Bailey hack to spend a good deal of his time down in the cells, in the basement area, where 20 they keep the old door of Newgate, kicked and scarred, through which generations of villains were sent to the tread-mill, the gallows or the whip. You pass this venerable door and ring a bell, you're let in and your name's taken by one of the warders who bring the prisoners from Brixton. There's a perpetual smell of cooking and the warders are snatching odd snacks of six inches of cheese butties and a gallon of tea. Lunch is being got ready, and the cells under the Bailey have a high reputation as one of the best caffs in London. By the door the screws have their pinups and comic cartoons of judges. You are taken to a waiting-room, three steel chairs and a table, and you meet the client. Perhaps he is a novice, making his first appearance, like Jim Timson. Perhaps he's an old hand asking anxiously which judge he's got, knowing their form as accurately as a betting-shop proprietor. Whoever he is, the client will be nervously excited, keyed up for his great day, full of absurd hope.

The worst part of a barrister's life at the Old Bailey is going back to the cells after a guilty verdict to say 'good-bye'. There's no purpose in it, but, as a point of honour, it has to be done. Even then the barrister probably gets the best reaction, and almost never any blame. The client is stunned, knocked out by his sentence. Only in a couple of weeks' time, when the reality of being banged up with the sour smell of stone walls and his own chamber-pot for company becomes apparent, does the convict start to weep. He is then drugged with sedatives, and Agatha Christies from the prison library.

When I saw the youngest Timson before his trial that morning, I couldn't help noticing how much smaller, and how much more experienced, he looked than my Nick. In his clean sports jacket and carefully knotted tie he was well dressed for the dock, and he showed all the carefully suppressed excitement of a young lad about to step into the limelight of Number One with an old judge, twelve jurors and a mixed bag of lawyers waiting to give him their undivided attention.

'Me speak to Peanuts? No Timson don't ever speak to a Molloy. It's a point of honour, like,' Jim added his voice to the family chorus.

'Since the raid on the Streatham Co-op. Your grandfather?'

'Dad told you about that, did he?'

'Yes. Dad told me.'

'Well, Dad wouldn't let me speak to no Molloy. He wouldn't put up with it, like.'

I stood up, grinding out the stub end of my small cigar in the old Oxo tin thoughtfully provided by HM's Government. It was, I thought, about time I called the meeting to order.

'So Jim,' I asked him, 'what's the defence?'

Little Jim knitted his brows and came out with his contribution. 'Well. I didn't do it.'

'That's an interesting defence. Somewhat novel – so far as the Timsons are concerned.'

'I've got my alibi, ain't I?'

Jim looked at me accusingly, as at an insensitive visitor to a garden who has failed to notice the remarkable display of gladioli.

'Oh, yes. Your alibi.' I'm afraid I didn't sound overwhelmed with enthusiasm.

'Dad reckoned it was pretty good.'

Mr Bernard had his invaluable file open and was reading from that less-than-inspiring document, our Notice of Alibi.

'Straight from school on that Friday September 2nd, I went up to tea at my Aunty Doris's and arrived there at exactly 5.30. At 6 p.m. my Uncle Den came home from work accompanied by my Uncle Cyril. At 7 p.m. when this alleged crime was taking place I was sat round the television with my Aunty and two Uncles. I well remember we was watching *The Newcomers*.'

All very neat and workmanlike. Well, that was it. The family gave young Jim an alibi, clubbed together for it, like a new bicycle. However, I had to disappoint Mr Bernard about the bright shining alibi and we went through the swing doors on our way into court.

'We can't use that alibi.'

'We can't?' Mr Bernard looked wounded, as if I'd just insulted his favourite child.

'Think about it, Bernard. Don't be blinded by the glamour of the criminal classes. Call the Uncles and the Aunties? Let them all be cross-examined about their records? The jury'll realize our Jimbo comes from a family of villains who keep a cupboard full of alibis for all occasions.'

Mr Bernard was forced to agree, but I went into my old place in court (nearest to the jury, furthest from the witness-box) thinking that the devilish thing about that impossible alibi was that it might even be true.

So there I was, sitting in my favourite seat in court, down in the firing line, and there was Jim boy, undersized for a 23 prisoner, just peeping over the edge of the dock, guarded in case he ran amok and started attacking the judge, by a huge dock officer. There was the jury, solid and grey, listening dispassionately as Guthrie Featherstone spread out his glittering mass of incriminating facts before them. I don't know why it is that juries all look the same; take twelve good men and women off the street and they all look middle-aged, anonymous, slightly stunned, an average jury, of average people trying an average case. Perhaps being a jury has become a special profession for specially average people. 'What do you want to do when you grow up, my boy?' 'Be a jury man, Daddy.' 'Well done, my boy. You can work a five-hour day for reasonable expenses and occasionally send people to chokey.'

So, as the carefully chosen words of Guthrie Featherstone passed over our heads like expensive hair oil, and as the enthusiastic young MacLay noted it all down, and the Rumpole Supporters Club, the Timsons, sat and pursed their lips and now and then whispered, 'Lies. All lies to each other, I sat watching the judge rather as a noted toreador watches the bull from the barrier during the preliminary stages of the corrida, and remembered what I knew of Mr Justice Everglade, known to his few friends as 'Florrie'. Everglade's father was Lord Chancellor about the time when Jim's grandfather was doing over the Streatham Co-op. Educated at Winchester and Balliol, he always cracked the *Times* crossword in the opening of an egg. He was most happy with international trust companies suing each other on

nice points of law, and was only there for a fortnight's

slumming down the Old Bailey. I wondered exactly what he was going to make of Peanuts Molloy.

'Members of the Jury, it's right that you should know that it is alleged that Timson took part in this attack with a number of other youths, none of whom have been arrested,' Featherstone was purring to a halt.

'"The boy stood on the burning deck whence all but he had fled,"' I muttered, but the judge was busy congratulating learned counsel for Her Majesty the Queen who was engaged that morning in prosecuting the pride of the Timsons.

'It is quite right you should tell the jury that, Mr Featherstone. Perfectly right and proper.'

'If your Lordship pleases.' Featherstone was now bowing slightly, and my hackles began to rise. What was this? The old chums' league? Fellow members of the Athenaeum?

'I am most grateful to your Lordship for that indication.' Featherstone did his well-known butler passing the sherry act again. I wondered why the old darling didn't crawl up on the Bench with Mr Justice Everglade and black his boots for him.

'So I imagine this young man's defence is – he wasn't *ejusdem generis* with the other lads?' The judge was now holding a private conversation, a mutual admiration society with my learned friend. I decided to break it up, and levered myself to my feet.

'I'm sorry. Your Lordship was asking about the defence?'

The judge turned an unfriendly eye on me and fumbled for my name. I told you he was a stranger to the Old Bailey, where the name of Rumpole is, I think, tolerably well known. 25

'Yes, Mr . . . er . . .' The clerk of the court handed him up a note on which the defender's name was inscribed. 'Rumpole.'

'I am reluctant to intrude on your Lordship's confidential conversation with my learned friend. But your Lordship was asking about the defence.'

'You are appearing for the young man . . . Timson?'

'I have that honour.'

At which point the doors of the court swung open and Albert came in with Nick, a boy in a blazer and a school tie who passed the boy in the dock with only a glance of curiosity. I always thank God, when I consider the remote politeness with which I was treated by the Reverend Wilfred Rumpole, that I get on extremely well with Nick. We understand each other, my boy and I, and have, when he's at home, formed a strong but silent alliance against the almost invincible rule of She Who Must Be Obeyed. He is as fond as I am of the Sherlock Holmes tales, and when we walked together in Hyde Park and Kensington Gardens, young Nick often played the part of Holmes whilst I trudged beside him as Watson, trying to deduce the secret lives of those we passed by the way they shined their shoes, or kept their handkerchiefs in their sleeves. So I gave a particularly welcoming smile to Nick before I gave my attention back to Florrie.

'And, as Jim Timson's counsel,' I told his Lordship, 'I might know a little more about his case than counsel for the prosecution.'

To which Mr Justice Everglade trotted out his favourite

bit of Latin. 'I imagine,' he said loftily, 'your client says he was not *ejusdem generis* with the other lads.'

'*Ejusdem generis?* Oh yes, my Lord. He's always saying that. *Ejusdem generis* is a phrase in constant use in his particular part of Brixton.'

I had hit a minor jackpot, and was rewarded with a tinkle of laughter from the Timsons, and a smile of genuine congratulation from Nick.

Mr Justice Everglade was inexperienced down the Bailey – he gave us a bare hour for lunch and Nick and I had it in the canteen. There is one thing you can say against crime, the catering facilities aren't up to much. Nick told me about school, and freely confessed, as I'm sure he wouldn't have done to his mother, that he'd been in some sort of trouble that term. There was an old deserted vicarage opposite Schoolhouse and he and his friends had apparently broken in the scullery window and assembled there for poker parties and the consumption of cherry brandy. I was horrified as I drew up the indictment which seemed to me to contain charges of Burglary at Common Law, House Breaking under the Forcible Entries Act, contravening the Betting, Gaming, Lotteries Act and Serving Alcohol on Unlicensed Premises.

'Crabtree actually invited a couple of girls from the village,' Nick continued his confession. 'But Bagnold never got to hear of that.'

Bagnold was Nick's headmaster, the school equivalent of 'Persil' White. I cheered up a little at the last piece of information.

'Then there's no evidence of girls. As far as your case goes there's no reason to suppose the girls ever existed. As for the other charges, which are serious . . .'

'Yes, yes, I suppose they are rather.'

'I imagine you were walking past the house on Sunday evening and, attracted by the noise . . . You went to investigate?'

'Dad. Bagnold came in and found us – playing poker.'

Nick wasn't exactly being helpful. I tried another line.

'I know, "My Lord. My client was only playing poker in order not to look too pious whilst he lectured his fellow sixth formers on the evils of gambling and cherry brandy".'

'Dad. Be serious.'

'I am serious. Don't you want me to defend you?'

'No. Bagnold's not going to tell the police or anything like that.'

I was amazed. 'He isn't? What's he going to do?'

'Well . . . I'll miss next term's exeat. Do extra work. I thought I should tell you before you got a letter.'

'Thank you, Nick. Thank you. I'm glad you told me. So there's no question of . . . the police?'

'The police?' Nick was laughing. 'Of course not. Bagnold doesn't want any trouble. After all, we're still at school.'

I watched Nick as he finished his fish and chips, and then turned my thoughts to Jim Timson, who had also been at school, but with no kindly Bagnold to protect him.

Back in court I was cross-examining that notable grass, Peanuts Molloy, a skinnier, more furtive edition of Jim

Timson. The cross-examination was being greatly enjoyed by the Timsons and Nick, but not much by Featherstone or Chief Detective Inspector Persil White who sat at the table in front of me. I also thought that Mr Justice Florrie Everglade was thinking that he would have been happier snoozing in the Athenaeum, or working on his *grospoint* in Egerton Terrace, than listening to me bowling fast inswingers at the juvenile chief witness for the prosecution.

'You don't speak. The Molloys and the Timsons are like the Montagues and the Capulets,' I put it to Peanuts.

'What did you say they were?' The judge had, of course, given me my opportunity. I smacked him through the slips for a crafty single. 'Not *ejusdem generis*, my Lord,' I said.

Nick joined in the laughter and even the ranks of Featherstone had to stifle a smile. The usher called 'Silence'. We were back to the business in hand.

'Tell me, Peanuts . . . How would you describe yourself?'

'Is that a proper question?' Featherstone uncoiled himself gracefully. I ignored the interruption.

'I mean artistically. Are you a latter-day Impressionist? Do all your oils in little dots, do you? Abstract painter? White squares on a white background? Do you indulge in watches melting in the desert like dear old Salvador Dali?'

'I don't know what you're talking about.' Peanuts played a blocking shot and Featherstone tried a weary smile to the judge.

'My Lord, neither, I must confess, do I.'

'Sit quietly, Featherstone,' I muttered to him. 'All will be revealed to you.' I turned my attention back to Peanuts. 'Are 29 you a dedicated artist? The Rembrandt of the remand centre?'

'I hadn't done no art before.' Peanuts confirmed my suspicions.

'So we are to understand that this occasion, when Jim poured out his heart to you, was the first painting lesson you'd ever been to?'

Peanuts admitted it.

'You'd been at the remand centre how long?'

'Couple of months. I was done for a bit of an affray.'

'I didn't ask you that. And I'm sure the reason you were on remand was entirely creditable. What I want to know is, what inspired you with this sudden fascination for the arts?'

'Well, the chief screw. He suggested it.'

Now we were beginning to get to the truth of the matter. Like his old grandfather in the Streatham Co-op days, Jim had been banged up with a notable grass.

'You were suddenly told to join the painting class, weren't you . . . and put yourself next to Jim?'

'Something like that, yeah.'

'What did he say?' Florrie frowned. It was all very strange to him and yet he was starting to get the hint of something that wasn't quite cricket.

'Something like that, my Lord,' I repeated slowly, giving the judge a chance to make a note. 'And you were sent there, not in the pursuit of art, Peanuts, but in the pursuit of evidence! You knew that and you supplied your masters with just what they wanted to hear – even though Jim Timson didn't say a word to you!'

Everyone in court, including Nick, looked impressed. DI White bit hard on a polo mint and Featherstone oozed to his feet in a rescue bid.

'That's great, Dad!'

'Thanks, Nick. Sorry it's not a murder.'

'I don't know quite what my learned friend is saying. Is he suggesting that the police . . .'

'Oh, it's an old trick,' I said, staring hard at the Chief Inspector. 'Bang the suspect up with a notable grass when you're really pushed for evidence. They do it with grown-ups often enough. Now they're trying it with children!'

'Mr Rumpole,' the judge sighed, 'you are speaking a language which is totally foreign to me.'

'Let me try and make myself clear, my Lord. I was suggesting that Peanuts was put there as a deliberate trap.'

By now, even the judge had the point. 'You are suggesting that Mr Molloy was not a genuine "amateur painter"?'

'No, my Lord. Merely an amateur witness.'

'Yes.' I actually got a faint smile. 'I see. Please go on, Mr Rumpole.'

Another day or so of this, I felt, and I'd get invited to tea at the Athenaeum.

'What did you say first to Jim? As you drew your easel alongside?'

'Don't remember.'

'Don't you?'

'I think we was speaking about the Stones.'

'What "stones" are these?' The judge's ignorance of the life around him seemed to be causing him some sort of wild panic. Remember, this was 1965, and I was in a similar state of confusion until Nick, whispering from behind me, gave me the clue.

'The Rolling Stones, my Lord.' The information meant nothing to him.

'I'm afraid a great deal of this case seems to be taking place in a foreign tongue, Mr Rumpole.'

'Jazz musicians, as I understand it, my Lord, of some notoriety.' By courtesy of Nick, I filled his Lordship in on 'the scene'.

'Well, the notoriety hasn't reached me!' said the judge, providing the obedient Featherstone with the laugh of the year, if not the century. When the learned prosecuting counsel had recovered his solemnity, Peanuts went rambling on.

'We was talking about the Stones concert at the Hammersmith Odeon. We'd both been to it, like. And, well . . . we talked about that. And then he said . . . Jim said . . . Well, he said as how he and the other blokes had done the butchers.'

The conversation had now taken a nasty turn. I saw that the judge was writing industriously. 'Jim said . . . that he and the other blokes . . . had done the butchers.' Florrie was plying his pencil. Then he looked up at me, 'Well, Mr Rumpole, is that a convenient moment to adjourn?'

It was a very convenient moment for the prosecution, as the evidence against us would be the last thing the jury heard before sloping off to their homes and loved ones. It was also a convenient moment for Peanuts. He would have his second wind by the morning. So there was nothing for it but to take

Nick for a cup of tea and a pile of crumpets in the ABC, and so home to She Who Must Be Obeyed.

So picture us three that evening, finishing dinner and a bottle of claret, celebrating the return of the Young Master at Hack Hall, Counsel's Castle, Rumpole Manor, or 25B Froxbury Mansions, Gloucester Road. Hilda had told Nick that his grandpa had sent his love and expected a letter, and also dropped me the encouraging news that old C. H. Wystan was retiring and quite appreciated that I was the senior man. Nick asked me if I was really going to be Head of Chambers, seeming to look at me with a new respect, and we drank a glass of claret to the future, whatever it might be. Then Nick asked me if I really thought Peanuts Molloy was lying.

'If he's not, he's giving a damn good imitation.' Then I told Hilda as she started to clear away, 'Nick enjoyed the case. Even though it was only a robbery. Oh, Nick . . . I wish you'd been there to hear me cross-examine about the blood-stains in the Penge Bungalow Murders.'

'Nick wasn't born when you did the Penge Bungalow Murders.'

My wife is always something of a wet blanket. I commiserated with my son. 'Bad luck, old boy.'

'You were great with that judge!'

I think Nick had really enjoyed himself.

'There was this extraordinary judge who was always talking Latin and Dad was teasing him.'

'You want to be careful,' Hilda was imposing her will on the pudding plates. 'How you tease judges. If you're to be

Head of Chambers.' On which line she departed, leaving Nick and me to our claret and conversation. I began to discuss with Nick the horrifying adventure of *The Speckled Band*.

'You're still reading those tales, are you?' I asked Nick.

'Well . . . not lately.'

'But you remember. I used to read them to you, didn't I? After She had ordered you to bed.'

'When you weren't too busy. Noting up your murders.'

'And remember we were Holmes and Watson? When we went for walks in Hyde Park.'

'I remember *one* walk.'

That was odd, as I recall it had been our custom ever at a weekend, before Nick went away to boarding school. I lit a small cigar and looked at the Great Detective through the smoke.

'Tell me, Holmes. What did you think was the most remarkable piece of evidence given by the witness Peanuts Molloy?'

'When he said they talked about the Rolling Stones.'

'Holmes, you astonish me.'

'You see, Watson, we were led to believe they were such enemies – I mean, the families were. They'd never spoken.'

'I see what you're driving at. Have another glass of claret – stimulates the detective ability.' I opened another bottle, a clatter from the kitchen telling me that the lady was not about to join us.

'And there they were chatting about a pop concert. Didn't
34 that strike you as strange, my dear Watson?'

'It struck me as bloody rum, if you want to know the truth, Holmes.' I was delighted to see Nick taking over the case.

'They'd both been to the concert . . . Well, that doesn't mean anything. Not necessarily . . . I mean, *I* was at that concert.'

'Were you indeed?'

'It was at the end of the summer holidays.'

'I don't remember you mentioning it.'

'I said I was going to the Festival Hall.'

I found this confidence pleasing, knowing that it wasn't to be shared with Hilda.

'Very wise. Your mother no doubt feels that at the Hammersmith Odeon they re-enact some of the worst excesses of the Roman Empire. You didn't catch sight of Peanuts and young Jimbo, did you?'

'There were about two thousand fans – all screaming.'

'I don't know if it helps . . .'

'No.'

'If they were old mates, I mean. Jim might really have confided in him. All the same, Peanuts is lying. And *you* noticed it! You've got the instinct, Nick. You've got a nose for the evidence! Your career at the Bar is bound to be brilliant.' I raised my glass to Nick. 'When are you taking silk?'

Shortly after this She entered with news that Nick had a dentist's appointment the next day, which would prevent his re-appearance down the Bailey. All the same, he had given me a great deal of help and before I went to bed I telephoned

Bernard the solicitor, tore him away from his fireside and instructed him to undertake some pretty immediate research.

Next morning, Albert told me that he'd had a letter from old C. H. Wystan, Hilda's Daddy, mentioning his decision to retire.

'I think we'll manage pretty well, with you, Mr Rumpole, as Head of Chambers,' Albert told me. 'There's not much you and I won't be able to sort out, sir, over a glass or two in Pommeroy's Wine Bar ... And soon we'll be welcoming Master Nick in chambers?'

'Nick? Well, yes.' I had to admit it. 'He is showing a certain legal aptitude.'

'It'll be a real family affair, Mr Rumpole ... Like father, like son, if you want my opinion.'

I remembered Albert's words when I saw Fred Timson waiting for me outside the court. But before I had time to brood on family tradition, Bernard came up with the rolled-up poster for a pop concert. I grabbed it from him and carried it as unobtrusively as possible into court.

'When Jim told you he'd done up the butchers ... He didn't tell you the date that that had happened?' Peanuts was back, facing the bowling, and Featherstone was up to his usual tricks, rising to interrupt.

'My Lord, the date is set out quite clearly in the indictment.'

The time had come, quite obviously, for a burst of right-
eous indignation.

'My Lord, I am cross-examining on behalf of a sixteen-year-old boy on an extremely serious charge. I'd be grateful if my learned friend didn't supply information which all of us in court know – except for the witness.'

'Very well. Do carry on, Mr Rumpole.' I was almost beginning to like Mr Justice Everglade.

'No. He never told me when, like. I thought it was some time in the summer.' Peanuts tried to sound co-operative.

'Sometime in the summer? Are you a fan of the Rolling Stones, Peanuts?'

'Yes.'

'Remind me . . . they were . . .' Still vaguely puzzled, the judge was hunting back through his notes.

Sleek as a butler with a dish of peas, Featherstone supplied the information. 'The musicians, my Lord.'

'And so was Jim a fan?' I ploughed on, ignoring the gentleman's gentleman.

'He was. Yes.'

'You had discussed music before you met in the remand centre?'

'Before the Nick. Oh yes.' Peanuts was following me obediently down the garden path.

'You used to talk about it at school?'

'Yes.'

'In quite a friendly way?' I was conscious of a startled Fred Timson looking at his son, and of Jim in the dock looking, for the first time, ashamed.

'We was all right. Yes.'

'Did you ever go to a concert with Jimbo? Please think carefully.'

'We went to one or two concerts together,' Peanuts conceded.

'In the evening?'

'Yes.'

'What would you do? . . . Call at his home and collect him?'

'You're joking!'

'Oh no, Peanuts. In this case I'm not joking at all!' No harm, I thought, at that stage, in underlining the seriousness of the occasion.

''Course I wouldn't call at his home!'

'Your families don't speak. You wouldn't be welcomed in each other's houses?'

'The Montagues and the Capulets, Mr Rumpole?' The old sweetheart on the Bench had finally got the message. I gave him a bow, to show my true love and affection.

'If your Lordship pleases . . . Your Lordship puts it extremely aptly.' I turned back to Peanuts. 'So what would you do, if you were going to a concert?'

'We'd leave school together, like – and then hang around the caffs.'

'Hang around the caffs?'

'Caf*ays*, Mr Rumpole?' Mr Justice Everglade was enjoying himself, translating the answer.

'Yes, of course, the caf*ays*. Until it was time to go up West? If my Lord would allow me, up to the "West End of London" together?'

'Yes.'

'So you wouldn't be separated on these evenings you went to concerts together?' It was one of those questions after which you hold your breath. There can be so many wrong answers.

'No. We hung around together.'

Rumpole breathed a little more easily, but he still had the final question, the great gamble, with all Jim Timson's chips firmly piled on the red. *Faîtes vos jeux, m'sieurs et mesdames* of the Old Bailey Jury. I spun the wheel.

'And did that happen . . . when you went to the Rolling Stones at the Hammersmith Odeon?'

A nasty silence. Then the ball rattled into the hole.

Peanuts said, 'Yes.'

'That was this summer, wasn't it?' We were into the straight now, cantering home.

'In the summer, yeah.'

'You left school together?'

'And hung around the caffs, like. Then we went up the Odeon.'

'Together . . . All the time?'

'I told you – didn't I?' Peanuts looked bored, and then amazed as I unrolled the poster Bernard had brought, rushed by taxi from Hammersmith, with the date clearly printed across the bottom.

'My Lord. My learned friend might be interested to know the date of the only Rolling Stones concert at the Hammersmith Odeon this year.' I gave Featherstone an unwelcome eyeful of the poster.

'He might like to compare it with the date so conveniently set out in the indictment.'

When the subsequent formalities were over, I went down to the cells. This was not a visit of commiseration, no time for a 'Sorry old sweetheart, but . . .' and a deep consciousness of having asked one too many questions. All the same, I was in no gentle mood, in fact, it would be fair to say that I was bloody angry with Jimbo.

'You had an alibi! You had a proper, reasonable, truthful alibi, and, joy of joys, it came from the prosecution! Why the hell didn't you tell me?'

Jim, who seemed to have little notion of the peril he had passed, answered me quite calmly, 'Dad wouldn't've liked it.'

'Dad! What's Dad got to do with it?' I was astonished.

'He wouldn't've liked it, Mr Rumpole. Not me going out with Peanuts.'

'So you were quite ready to be found guilty, to be convicted of robbery, just because your Dad wouldn't like you going out with Peanuts Molloy?'

'Dad got the family to alibi me.' Jim clearly felt that the Timsons had done their best for him.

'Keep it in the family!' Though it was heavily laid on, the irony was lost on Jim. He smiled politely and stood up, eager to join the clan upstairs.

'Well, anyway. Thanks a lot, Mr Rumpole. Dad said I could rely on you. To win the day, like. I'd better collect me things.'

If Jim thought I was going to let him get away as easily as that, he was mistaken. Rumpole rose in his crumpled gown, doing his best to represent the majesty of the law. 'No! Wait a minute. I didn't win the day. It was luck. The purest fluke. It won't happen again!'

'You're joking, Mr Rumpole.' Jim thought I was being modest. 'Dad told me about you . . . He says you never let the Timsons down.'

I had a sudden vision of my role in life, from young Jim's point of view, and I gave him the voice of outrage which I use frequently in court. I had a message of importance for Jim Timson.

'Do you think that's what I'm here for? To help you along in a career like your Dad's?' Jim was still smiling, maddeningly. 'My God! I shouldn't have asked those questions! I shouldn't have found out the date of the concert! Then you'd really be happy, wouldn't you? You could follow in Dad's footsteps all your life! Sharp spell of Borstal training to teach you the mysteries of house breaking, and then a steady life in the Nick. You might really do well! You might end up in Parkhurst maximum security wing, doing a glamorous twenty years and a hero to the screws.'

At which the door opened and a happy screw entered, for the purpose of springing young Jim – until the inevitable next time.

'We've got his things at the gate, Mr Rumpole. Come on, Jim. You can't stay here all night.'

'I've got to go,' Jim agreed. 'I don't know how to face Dad, really. Me being so friendly with Peanuts.'

41

'Jim,' I tried a last appeal. 'If you're at all grateful for what I did . . .'

'Oh, I am, Mr Rumpole, I'm quite satisfied.' Generous of him.

'Then you can perhaps repay me.'

'Why – aren't you on legal aid?'

'It's not that! Leave him! Leave your Dad.'

Jim frowned, for a moment he seemed to think it over. Then he said, 'I don't know as how I can.'

'You don't know?'

'Mum depends on me, you see. Like when Dad goes away. She depends on me then, as head of the family.'

So he left me, and went up to temporary freedom and his new responsibilities.

My mouth was dry and I felt about ninety years old, so I took the lift up to that luxurious eatery, the Old Bailey canteen, for a cup of tea and a Penguin biscuit. And, pushing his tray along past the urns, I met a philosophic Chief Inspector Persil White. He noticed my somewhat lugubrious expression and tried a cheering 'Don't look so miserable, Mr Rumpole. You won, didn't you?'

'Nobody won, the truth emerges sometimes, Inspector, even down the Old Bailey.' I must have sounded less than gracious. The wily old copper smiled tolerantly.

'He's a Timson. It runs in the family. We'll get him sooner or later!'

'Yes. Yes. I suppose you will.'

At a table in a corner, I found certain members of my

chambers, George Frobisher, Percy Hoskins, and young Tony MacLay, now resting from their labours, their wigs lying among cups of Old Bailey tea, buns and choccy bics. I joined them. Wordsworth entered my head, and I gave him an airing: ' "Trailing clouds of glory do we come." '

'Marvellous win, that. I was telling them.' Young MacLay thought I was announcing my triumph.

'Yes, Rumpole. I hear you've had a splendid win.' Old George, ever generous, smiled, genuinely pleased.

'It'll be *years* before you get the cheque,' Hoskins grumbled.

> 'Not in entire forgetfulness,
> And not in utter nakedness,
> But trailing clouds of glory do we come
> From God, who is our home.'

I was thinking of Jim, trying to sort out his situation with the help of Wordsworth.

'You don't get paid for years at the Old Bailey. I try to tell my grocer that. If you had to wait as long to be paid for a pound of sugar, I tell him, as we do for an Armed Robbery . . .' Hoskins was warming to a well-loved theme, but George, dear old George, was smiling at me.

'Albert tells me he's had a letter from Wystan. I just wanted to say, I'm sure we'd all like to say, you'll make a splendid Head of Chambers, Rumpole.'

> 'Heaven lies about us in our infancy!
> Shades of the prison-house begin to close

43

Upon the growing boy,
But he beholds the light, and whence it flows,
He sees it in his joy.'

I gave them another brief glimpse of immortality. George looked quite proud of me and told MacLay, 'Rumpole quotes poetry. He does it quite often.'

'But does the growing boy behold the light?' I wondered. 'Or was the old sheep of the Lake District being unduly optimistic?'

'It'll be refreshing for us all, to have a Head of Chambers who quotes poetry,' George went on, at which point Percy Hoskins produced a newspaper which turned out to contain an item of news for us all.

'Have you seen *The Times*, Rumpole?'

'No, I haven't had time for the crossword.'

'Guthrie Featherstone. He's taken silk.'

It was the apotheosis, the great day for the Labour-Conservative Member for wherever it was, one-time unsuccessful prosecutor of Jim Timson and now one of Her Majesty's counsel, called within the Bar, and he went down to the House of Lords tailored out in his new silk gown, a lace jabot, knee breeches with *diamanté* buckles, patent shoes, black silk stockings, lace cuffs and a full-bottomed wig that made him look like a pedigree, but not over-bright, spaniel. However, Guthrie Featherstone was a tall man, with a good calf in a silk stocking, and he took with him Marigold, his lady wife, who was young enough, and I suppose pretty enough, for Henry our junior clerk to eye wistfully, although she had the sort of voice that puts me instantly in mind of headscarves and gymkhanas, that high-pitched nasal whining which a girl learns from too much contact with the saddle when young, and too little with the Timsons of this world in later life. The couple were escorted by Albert, who'd raided Moss Bros for a top hat and morning coat for the occasion, and when the Lord Chancellor had welcomed Guthrie to that special club of Queen's Counsel (on whose advice the Queen, luckily for her, never has to rely for a moment) they came back to chambers where champagne (the NV cooking variety, bulk-bought from Pommeroy's Wine Bar) was served by Henry and old Miss Patterson our typist, in Wystan's big room looking out over Temple Gardens. C. H. Wystan, our retiring Head, was not among those present as the party began, and I took an early opportunity to get stuck into the beaded bubbles.

After the fourth glass I felt able to relax a bit and wandered to where Featherstone, in all his finery, was holding forth to Erskine-Brown about the problems of appearing *en travesti*. I arrived just as he was saying, 'It's the stockings that're the problem.'

'Oh yes. They would be.' I did my best to sound interested.

'Keeping them up.'

'I do understand.'

'Well, Marigold. My wife Marigold . . .' I looked across to where Mrs QC was tinkling with laughter at some old legal anecdote of Uncle Tom's. It was a laugh that seemed in some slight danger of breaking the wine glasses.

'*That* Marigold?'

'Her sister's a nurse, you know . . . and she put me in touch with this shop which supplies suspender belts to nurses . . . among other things.'

'Really?' This conversation seemed to arouse some dormant sexual interest in Erskine-Brown.

'Yards of elastic, for the larger ward sister. But it works miraculously.'

'You're wearing a suspender belt?' Erskine-Brown was frankly fascinated. 'You sexy devil!'

'I hadn't realized the full implications,' I told the QC, 'of rising to the heights of the legal profession.'

I wandered off to where Uncle Tom was giving Marigold a brief history of life in our chambers over the last half-century. Percy Hoskins was in attendance, and George.

'It's some time since we had champagne in chambers.' Uncle Tom accepted a refill from Albert.

'It's some time since we had a silk in chambers,' Hoskins smiled at Marigold who flashed a row of well-groomed teeth back at him.

'I recall we had a man in chambers once called Drinkwater – oh, before you were born, Hoskins. And some fellow came and paid Drinkwater a hundred guineas – for six months' pupillage. And you know what this Drinkwater fellow did? Bought us all champagne – and the next day he ran off to Calais with his junior clerk. We never saw hide nor hair of either of them again.' He paused. Marigold looked puzzled, not quite sure if this was the punch line.

'Of course, you could get a lot further in those days – on a hundred guineas,' Uncle Tom ended on a sad note, and Marigold laughed heartily.

'Your husband's star has risen so quickly, Mrs Featherstone. Only ten years' call and he's an MP *and* leading counsel.' Hoskins was clearly so excited by the whole business he had stopped worrying about his cheques for half an hour.

'Oh, it's the PR, you know. Guthrie's frightfully good at the PR.'

I felt like Everglade. Marigold was speaking a strange and incomprehensible language.

'Guthrie always says the most important thing at the Bar is to be polite to your instructing solicitor. Don't you find that, Mr Rumpole?'

'Polite to solicitors? It's never occurred to me.'

'Guthrie admires you so, Mr Rumpole. He admires your style of advocacy.'

I had just sunk another glass of the beaded bubbles as passed by Albert, and I felt a joyous release from my usual strong sense of tact and discretion.

'I suppose it makes a change from bowing three times and offering to black the judge's boots for him.'

Marigold's smile didn't waver. 'He says you're most amusing out of court, too. Don't you quote poetry?'

'Only in moments of great sadness, madam. Or extreme elation.'

'Guthrie's so looking forward to leading you. In his next big case.'

This was an eventuality which I should have taken into

account as soon as I saw Guthrie in silk stockings; as a matter of fact it had never occurred to me.

'Leading *me*? Did you say, *leading* me?'

'Well, he has to have a junior now . . . doesn't he? Naturally he wants the best junior available.'

'Now he's a leader?'

'Now he's left the Junior Bar.'

I raised my glass and gave Marigold a version of Browning. 'Just for a pair of knee breeches he left us . . . Just for an elastic suspender belt, as supplied to the nursing profession . . .' At which the QC himself bore down on us in a rustle of silk and drew me into a corner.

'I just wanted to say, I don't see why recent events should make the slightest difference to the situation in chambers. You *are* the senior man in practice, Rumpole.'

Henry was passing with the fizzing bottle. I held out my glass and the tide ran foaming in it.

'"You wrong me, Brutus,"' I told Featherstone. '"I said an elder soldier, not a better."'

'A quotation! *Touché*, very apt.'

'Is it?'

'I mean, all this will make absolutely no difference. I'll still support you, Rumpole, as the right candidate for Head of Chambers.'

I didn't know about being a candidate, having thought of the matter as settled and not being much of a political animal. But before I had time to reflect on whatever the Honourable Member was up to, the door opened letting in a formidable draught and the Head of Chambers C. H. Wystan,

48

She's Daddy, wearing a tweed suit, extremely pale, supported by Albert on one side and a stick on the other, made the sort of formidable entrance that the ghost of Banquo stages at dinner with the Macbeths. Wystan was installed in an armchair, from which he gave us all the sort of wintry smile which seemed designed to indicate that all flesh is as the grass, or something to that effect.

'Albert wrote to me about this little celebration. I was determined to be with you. And the doctor has given permission, for no more than one glass of champagne.' Wystan held out a transparent hand into which Albert inserted a glass of non-vintage. Wystan lifted this with some apparent effort, and gave us a toast.

'To the great change in chambers! Now we have a silk. Guthrie Featherstone, QC, MP!'

I had a large refill to that. Wystan absorbed a few bubbles, wiped his mouth on a clean, folded handkerchief, and proceeded to the oration. Wystan was never a great speech maker, but I claimed another refill and gave him my ears.

'You, Featherstone, have brought a great distinction to chambers.'

'Isn't that nice, Guthrie?' Marigold proprietorially squeezed her master's fingers.

'You know, when I was a young man. You remember when we were young men, Uncle Tom? We used to hang around in chambers for weeks on end.' Wystan had gone on about these distant hard times at every chambers meeting. 'I well recall we used to occupy ourselves with an old golf ball 49 and mashie-niblick, trying to get chip shots into the waste-paper baskets. Albert was a boy then.'

'A mere child, Mr Wystan.' Albert looked suitably demure.

'And we used to pray for work. *Any* sort of work, didn't we, Uncle Tom?'

'We were tempted to crime. Only way we could get into court.' Uncle Tom took the feed line like a professional. Moderate laughter, except for Rumpole who was busy drinking. And then I heard Wystan rambling on.

'But as you grow older at the Bar you discover it's not having any work that matters. It's the *quality* that counts!'

'Hear, hear! I'm always saying we ought to do more civil.' This was the dutiful Erskine-Brown, inserting his oar.

'Now Guthrie Featherstone, QC, MP, will, of course, command briefs in all divisions – planning, contract,' Wystan's voice sank to a note of awe, 'even Chancery! I was so afraid, after I've gone, that this chambers might become known as merely a criminal set.' Wystan's voice now sank in a sort of horror. 'And, of course, there's no doubt about it, too much criminal work does rather lower the standing of a chambers.'

'Couldn't you install pit-head baths?' I hadn't actually meant to say it aloud, but it came out very loud indeed.

'Ah, Horace.' Wystan turned his pale eyes on me for the first time.

'So we could have a good scrub down after we get back from the Old Bailey?'

'Now, Horace Rumpole. And I mean no disrespect what-ever to my son-in-law.' Wystan returned to the oration.

From far away I heard myself say, 'Daddy!' as I raised the hard-working glass. 'Horace does practise almost exclusively in the criminal courts!'

'One doesn't get the really fascinating points of *law*. Not in criminal work,' Erskine-Brown was adding unwanted support to the motion. 'I've often thought we should try and attract some really lucrative tax cases into chambers.'

That, I'm afraid, did it. Just as if I were in court I moved slightly to the centre and began my speech.

'Tax cases?' I saw them all smiling encouragement at me. 'Marvellous! Tax cases make the world go round. Compared to the wonderful world of tax, crime is totally trivial. What does it matter? If some boy loses a year, a couple of years, of his life? It's totally unimportant! Anyway, he'll grow up to be banged up for a good five, shut up with his own chamber-pot in some convenient hole we all prefer not to think about.' There was a deafening silence, which came loudest from Marigold Featherstone. Then Wystan tried to reach a settlement.

'Now then, Horace. Your practice no doubt requires a good deal of skill.'

'Skill? Who said "skill"?' I glared round at the learned friends. 'Any fool could do it! It's only a matter of life and death. That's all it is. Crime? It's a sort of a game. How can you compare it to the real world of offshore securities. And deductible expenses?'

'All you young men in chambers can learn an enormous amount from Horace Rumpole, when it comes to crime.' Wystan now seemed to be the only one who was still smiling. I turned on him.

'You make me sound just like Fred Timson!'

'Really? Whoever's Fred Timson?' I told you Wystan never had much of a practice at the Bar, consequently he had never met the Timsons. Erskine-Brown supplied the information.

'The Timsons are Rumpole's favourite family.'

'An industrious clan of South London criminals, aren't they, Rumpole?' Hoskins added.

Wystan looked particularly pained. 'South London criminals?'

'I mean, do we want people like the Timsons forever hanging about in our waiting-room? I merely ask the question.' He was not bad, this Erskine-Brown, with a big future in the nastier sort of Breach of Trust cases.

'Do you? Do you merely ask it?' I heard the pained bellow of a distant Rumpole.

'The Timsons . . . and their like, are no doubt grist to Rumpole's mill,' Wystan was starting on the summing up. 'But it's the balance that *counts*. Now, you'll be looking for a new Head of Chambers.'

'Are we still looking?' my friend George Frobisher had the decency to ask. And Wystan told him, 'I'd like you all to think it over carefully. And put your views to me in writing. We should all try and remember, it's the good of the chambers that matters. Not the feelings, however deep they may be, of any particular person.'

He then called on Albert's assistance to raise him to his feet, lifted his glass with an effort of pure will and offered us
52 a toast to the good of chambers. I joined in, and drank deep,

it having been a good thirty seconds since I had had a glass to my lips. As the bubbles exploded against the tongue I noticed that the Featherstones were holding hands, and the brand new artificial silk was looking particularly delighted. Something, and perhaps not only his suspender belt, seemed to be giving him special pleasure.

Some weeks later, when I gave Hilda the news, she was deeply shocked.

'*Guthrie Featherstone*! Head of Chambers!' We were at breakfast. In fact Nick was due back at school that day. He was neglecting his cornflakes and reading a book.

'By general acclaim.'

'I'm sorry.' Hilda looked at me, as if she'd just discovered that I'd contracted an incurable disease.

'He can have the headaches – working out Albert's extra-ordinary book-keeping system.' I thought for a moment, yes, I'd like to have been Head of Chambers, and then put the thought from me.

'If only you could have become a QC.' She was now pouring me an unsolicited cup of coffee.

'QC? CT. That's enough to keep me busy.'

'CT? Whatever's CT?'

'Counsel for the Timsons!' I tried to say it as proudly as I could. Then I reminded Nick that I'd promised to see him off at Liverpool Street, finished my cooling coffee, stood up and took a glance at the book that was absorbing him, expecting it to be, perhaps, that spine-chilling adventure relating to the Footprints of an Enormous Hound. To my amazement the shocker in question was entitled simply *Studies in Sociology*.

'It's interesting.' Nick sounded apologetic.

'You astonish me.'

'Old Bagnold was talking about what I should read if I get into Oxford.'

'Of course you're going to read law, Nick. We're going to keep it in the family.' Hilda the barrister's daughter was clearing away deafeningly.

'I thought perhaps PPE and then go on to sociology.' Nick sounded curiously confident. Before Hilda could get in another word I made my position clear.

'PPE, that's very good, Nick! That's very good indeed! For God's sake. Let's stop keeping things in the family!'

Later, as we walked across the barren stretches of Liverpool Street station, with my son in his school uniform and me in my old striped trousers and black jacket, I tried to explain what I meant.

'That's what's wrong, Nick. That's the devil of it! They're being born around us all the time. Little Mr Justice Everglades . . . Little Timsons . . . Little Guthrie Featherstones. All being set off . . . to follow in father's footsteps.' We were at the barrier, shaking hands awkwardly. 'Let's have no more of that! No more following in father's footsteps. No more.'

Nick smiled, although I have no idea if he understood what I was trying to say. I'm not totally sure that I understood it either. Then the train removed him from me. I waved for a little, but he didn't wave back. That sort of thing is embarrass-
ing for a boy. I lit a small cigar and went by Tube to the

Bailey. I was doing a long firm fraud then; a particularly nasty business, out of which I got a certain amount of harmless fun.

PENGUIN 60s

are published on the occasion of Penguin's 60th anniversary

LOUISA MAY ALCOTT · *An Old-Fashioned Thanksgiving and Other Stories*

HANS CHRISTIAN ANDERSEN · *The Emperor's New Clothes*

J. M. BARRIE · *Peter Pan in Kensington Gardens*

WILLIAM BLAKE · *Songs of Innocence and Experience*

GEOFFREY CHAUCER · *The Wife of Bath and Other Canterbury Tales*

ANTON CHEKHOV · *The Black Monk* and *Peasants*

SAMUEL TAYLOR COLERIDGE · *The Rime of the Ancient Mariner*

COLETTE · *Gigi*

JOSEPH CONRAD · *Youth*

ROALD DAHL · *Lamb to the Slaughter and Other Stories*

ROBERTSON DAVIES · *A Gathering of Ghost Stories*

FYODOR DOSTOYEVSKY · *The Grand Inquisitor*

SIR ARTHUR CONAN DOYLE · *The Man with the Twisted Lip* and *The Adventure of the Devil's Foot*

RALPH WALDO EMERSON · *Nature*

OMER ENGLEBERT (TRANS.) · *The Lives of the Saints*

FANNIE FARMER · *The Original 1896 Boston Cooking-School Cook Book*

EDWARD FITZGERALD (TRANS.) · *The Rubáiyát of Omar Khayyám*

ROBERT FROST · *The Road Not Taken and Other Early Poems*

GABRIEL GARCÍA MÁRQUEZ · *Bon Voyage, Mr President and Other Stories*

NIKOLAI GOGOL · *The Overcoat* and *The Nose*

GRAHAM GREENE · *Under the Garden*

JACOB AND WILHELM GRIMM · *Grimm's Fairy Tales*

NATHANIEL HAWTHORNE · *Young Goodman Brown and Other Stories*

O. HENRY · *The Gift of the Magi and Other Stories*

WASHINGTON IRVING · *Rip Van Winkle* and *The Legend of Sleepy Hollow*

HENRY JAMES · *Daisy Miller*

V. S. VERNON JONES (TRANS.) · *Aesop's Fables*

JAMES JOYCE · *The Dead*

GARRISON KEILLOR · *Truckstop and Other Lake Wobegon Stories*

JACK KEROUAC · *San Francisco Blues*

STEPHEN KING · *Umney's Last Case*

RUDYARD KIPLING · *Baa Baa, Black Sheep* and *The Gardener*

LAO TZU · *Tao Te Ching*

D. H. LAWRENCE · *Love Among the Haystacks*

ABRAHAM LINCOLN · *The Gettysburg Address and Other Speeches*

JACK LONDON · *To Build a Fire and Other Stories*

HERMAN MELVILLE · *Bartleby* and *The Lightning-rod Man*

A. A. MILNE · *Winnie-the-Pooh and His Friends*

MICHEL DE MONTAIGNE · *Four Essays*

JOHN MORTIMER · *Rumpole and the Younger Generation*

THOMAS PAINE · *The Crisis*

DOROTHY PARKER · *Big Blonde and Other Stories*

EDGAR ALLAN POE · *The Pit and the Pendulum and Other Stories*

EDGAR ALLAN POE, AMBROSE BIERCE,
     AND ROBERT LOUIS STEVENSON · *Three Tales of Horror*

FRANKLIN DELANO ROOSEVELT · *Fireside Chats*

WILLIAM SHAKESPEARE · *Sixty Sonnets*

JOHN STEINBECK · *The Chrysanthemums and Other Stories*

PETER STRAUB · *Blue Rose*

PAUL THEROUX · *The Greenest Island*

HENRY DAVID THOREAU · *Walking*

JOHN THORN · *Baseball: Our Game*

LEO TOLSTOY · *Master and Man*

MARK TWAIN · *The Notorious Jumping Frog of Calaveras County*

H. G. WELLS · *The Time Machine*

EDITH WHARTON · *Madame de Treymes*

OSCAR WILDE · *The Happy Prince and Other Stories*

The Declaration of Independence and *The Constitution of the United States*

Mother Goose

The Revelation of St. John the Divine

Teachings of Jesus